Love Monster
& the Last Chocolate

Rachel Bright

HOLIDAY AIR

D1353984

HarperCollins *Children's Books*

This mOnster...
(Hello, LOVe Monster.)

...was just getting back
from his holiday.

And although it was a little bit
exciting to be home…he was sad to
leave his adventures behind him.

A BOX OF CHOCOLATES?

Just sitting there??
Waiting to be found???

LOVe MONster couldn't believe it !
You see...

EVeRYBODY knows

that mOnsters

SeRIOUSLY

LOVe

chOcolate.

Especially THIS mOnster.

His mouth started to water just thinking about what might be inside...

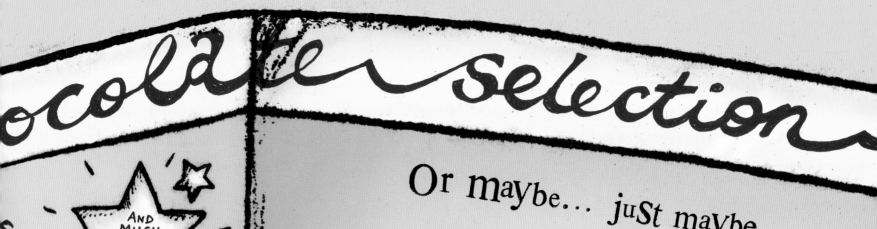

Explosion

...thbreaker

Tutti-frutti Splodge

AND MUCH MORE BESIDES!

...t Leaf

World's Chewiest Caramel Chew

...udge Button

Orange Bomb

Or maybe... just maybe... a

Double. Chocolate. Strawberry. Swirl.

Love Monster's absolute favourite!

But THEN he had a thought
that he just couldn't unthink.

Hmmmpf.

He should probably share the
chocolates with his friends,

BuT...

...what if there weren't enough?

Or...
what if someone
took the one

HE

wanted the most?

Or,
WORST
of all...

...what if the only one left for him was
THE COFFEE ONE??!

The Coffee One

EuUuuuRGGGHHh!

Everybody knows monsters HATE The Coffee One.

Especially THIs monster.

YuK!

Well,

I'm sorry to tell you
that after thinking all
of these thoughts,

Love Monster decided it would be

safer  and kinder

and better for everyone

 if he kept
the chocolates...

...just
for
himself.

So he went into
his house.

And so did
the box of
chocolates...

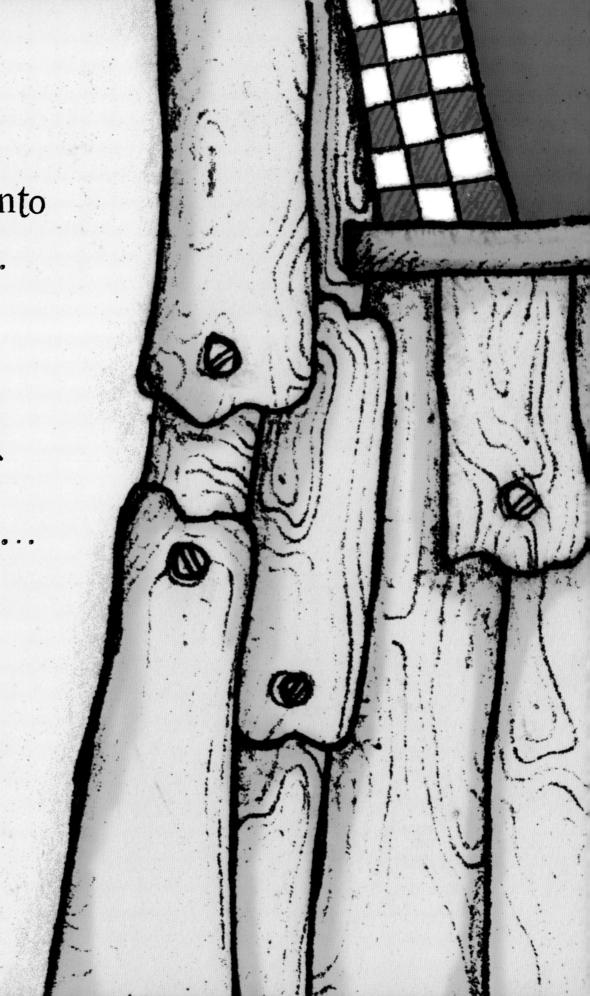

...without a whisper of a
word to anyone.

LOVE MONSTER
couldn't
WAIT!

Oh,
how his
mouth
watered.

But just as he went
to lift the lid,
he had a sort of
queasy-squeezy
feeling in
his heart.

It was
the feeling
a monster gets
when he knows
he is about to do
something he
Shouldn't...

And before you could say,
"Pass me the Truffle Surprise,"
he burst out of his house...

and **ran** as fast as his toes would carry him...

…to find his friends.

And when he did…
in a very **Out-of-breath-and-a-bit-shouty-Voice,**
he said,

"I GOT BACK FROM MY HOLIDAY AND I FOUND SOME CHOCOLATES AND I WAS GOING TO KEEP THEM ALL TO MYSELF BUT THEN I REALISED I WANTED TO SHARE THEM WITH YOU AND I DON'T EVEN WANT A SINGLE ONE

. . . well maybe one."

And do you know
what his friends said?

"Silly monster! Just open the box!"

You see, sometimes, it's when you stop to think of others...

...that you start to find out
just how much they think of you.

For Robbie
(The Wonderfulest Chocaholic I know)

THE
HOLIDAY
SOUVENIRS
FOR
FRIENDS
SHOP

And with
whizz-banger
thanks to
Mandy

First published in paperback in Great Britain by HarperCollins *Children's Books* in 2014

This edition published in 2020

5 7 9 10 8 6 4

ISBN: 978-0-00-754030-3

HarperCollins *Children's Books* is a division of HarperCollins*Publishers* Ltd.

Text and illustrations copyright © Rachel Bright 2014

Visit our website at: www.harpercollins.co.uk

Printed and bound in China